The Cooking Competition

T0328014

Written by Catherine Baker

Illustrated by Amy Lane

Collins

Who and what is in this story?

Listen and say

competition

prize

cake

🎧 Daisy and Jim were best friends.
They played in the playground at school.
They played at home and in the park, too!

Daisy liked running and singing.
Jim liked writing stories and playing
on the computer.

One day at school, Mrs Green told them about a cooking competition.

"There is a prize for the best cake and the best biscuits!" she said.

Jim looked at Daisy. Daisy looked at Jim.

Jim ran home after school. He told his mum about the competition.

"Don't worry! You can make some biscuits. It's easy!" his mum said.

Daisy told her dad about the competition, too.

"Can you help me make a cake, Dad?" she said.

"Yes! I like cooking with you!" said Dad.

Jim made the biscuits. He put everything in a big bowl. He added lots of chocolate!

Mum put the biscuits in the oven. The biscuits looked good!

Daisy made a big cake. She added lots of chocolate!

Dad put the cake in the oven. The cake looked good!

The kitchen was hot. Jim went into the garden.

Daisy wanted her cake to cook better.
She made the oven very hot.

Jim's biscuits were hard.

Daisy's cake was soft in the middle.
It looked terrible.

Daisy took her cake to Jim's house.
She saw Jim's hard biscuits. Then Daisy
had a clever idea!

"Let's make a big mix-up biscuit-cake!" said Daisy.

Daisy and Jim put the hard biscuits and the soft cake in a big bowl. They added more chocolate and they made some chocolate flowers.

Daisy and Jim took their mix-up biscuit-cake to school.

Mrs Green laughed when she saw the mix-up biscuit-cake.

"Yes! It's a biscuit and a cake!" said Daisy and Jim.

Ella got the prize for best cake. Mark got the prize for best biscuits.

But Daisy and Jim got a prize for the best mix-up biscuit-cake!

Best mix-up biscuit-cake!

Picture dictionary

Listen and repeat 3

biscuit

bowl

cake

hard

oven

soft

1 Look and order the story

2 Listen and say

Collins

Published by Collins
An imprint of HarperCollins*Publishers*
Westerhill Road
Bishopbriggs
Glasgow
G64 2QT

HarperCollins*Publishers*
1st Floor, Watermarque Building
Ringsend Road
Dublin 4
Ireland

William Collins' dream of knowledge for all began with the publication of his first book in 1819.

A self-educated mill worker, he not only enriched millions of lives, but also founded a flourishing publishing house. Today, staying true to this spirit, Collins books are packed with inspiration, innovation and practical expertise. They place you at the centre of a world of possibility and give you exactly what you need to explore it.

10 9 8 7 6 5 4 3 2

ISBN 978-0-00-839662-6

Collins® and COBUILD® are registered trademarks of HarperCollins*Publishers* Limited

www.collins.co.uk/elt

British Library Cataloguing in Publication Data

A catalogue record for this publication is available from the British Library.

Author: Catherine Baker
Illustrator: Amy Lane (Beehive)
Series editor: Rebecca Adlard
Commissioning editor: Zoë Clarke
Publishing manager: Lisa Todd
Product managers: Jennifer Hall and Caroline Green
In-house editor: Alma Puts Keren
Project manager: Emily Hooton
Editor: Barbara MacKay
Proofreaders: Natalie Murray and Michael Lamb
Cover designer: Kevin Robbins
Typesetter: 2Hoots Publishing Services Ltd
Audio produced by id audio, London
Reading guide author: Emma Wilkinson
Production controller: Rachel Weaver
Printed and bound by: GPS Group, Slovenia

Download the audio for this book and a reading guide for parents and teachers at www.collins.co.uk/839662